TINY
T. REX

AND THE GRAND TA-DA!

TALENT SHOW!

BE A STAR!

I want to try this, Tiny, but am I good enough?

I believe in you, Pointy.
We can do this. You and me!

TINY
T. REX

SCHOLASTIC INC.

AND THE GRAND TA-DA!

by Jonathan Stutzman   illustrated by Jay Fleck

Pointy and I will win the talent show. I know we can do it, because we both have many great skills.

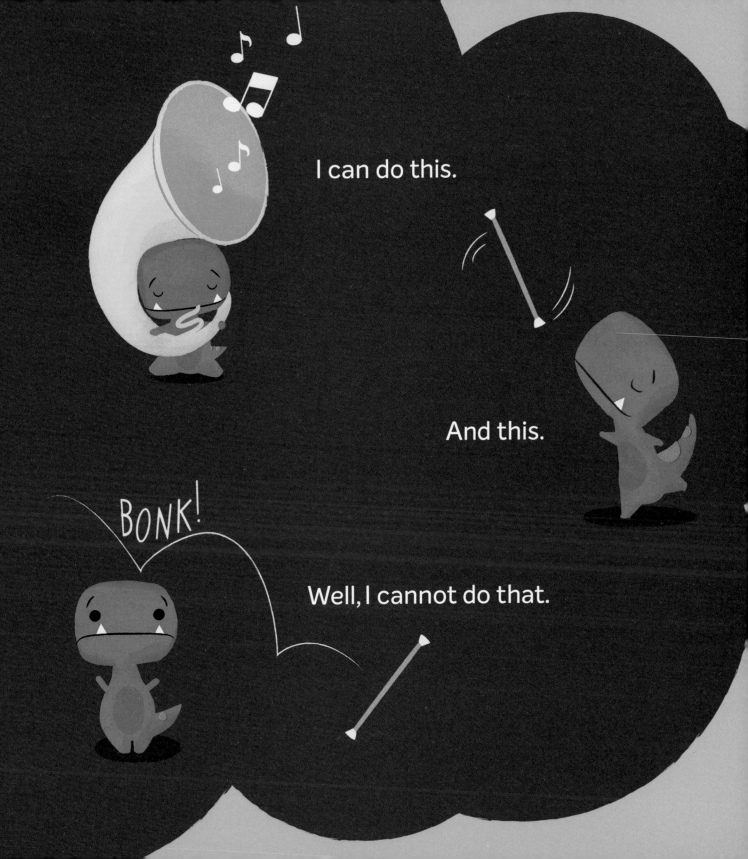

But Pointy can do that.

And that.

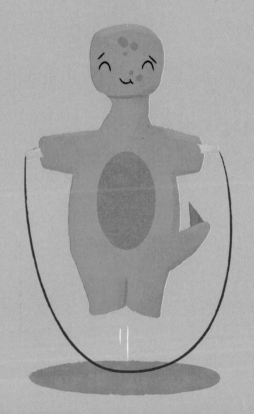

And that!

It is OK, Pointy. We cannot be good at everything by ourselves.

But we can be great at one thing together.

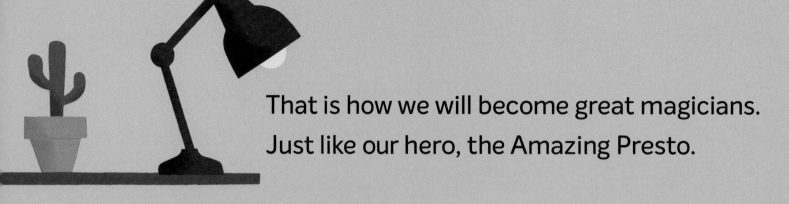

That is how we will become great magicians.
Just like our hero, the Amazing Presto.

The Amazing Presto says,

Magic is not for the magician alone.
Magic is meant to be shared.

Pointy and I will share our magic. We will stand
in the spotlight and do amazing things!

Dinosaurs everywhere will be
mesmerized by our fantastic feats!

And we will win the talent show with the grandest of tricks:

We will make something disappear.

But first, we must learn how to be magicians.

Magic hats are a good place to start. Every magician needs one to keep special secrets inside . . .

and to make them look extra-cool.

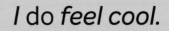

I do feel cool.

We also need magic
whooshes

and *swooshes*.

And our special assistant: Bob.

It is important for great magicians to learn magic words.
Words can be powerful when used correctly.

They help the audience know something
very special is about to happen.

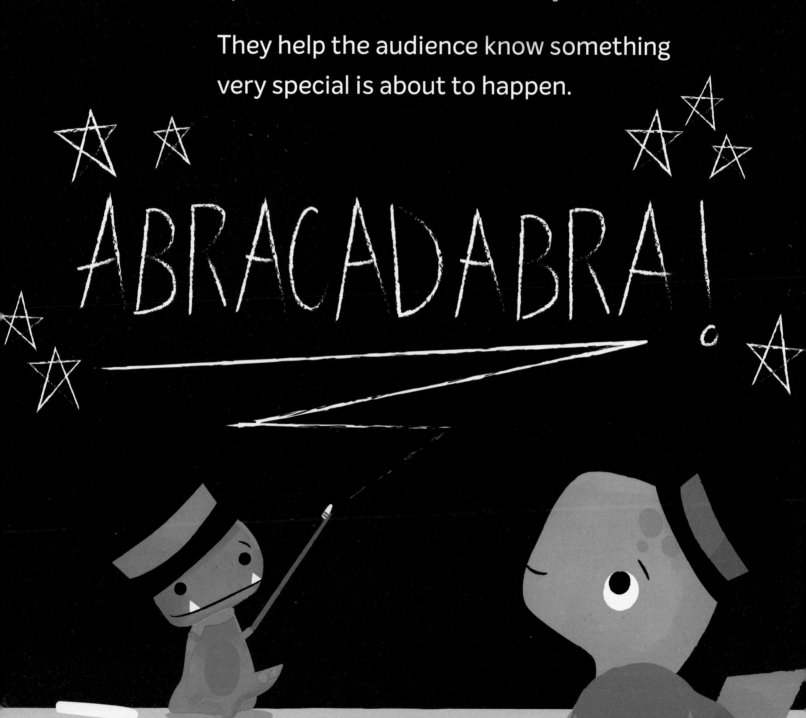

ABRACADABRA!

Learning magic words is tricky.

Abraca . . .

CHOO!

Abraca–bless you.

But all we need is one magic word.
Even if it is teeny.

Are you ready?

Three. Two. One.

TA–DA!

Perfect! We will say it when we
make something disappear.

Now that we talk like
real magicians,
we will practice our
grandest trick on Bob.

Three.   Two.   One.

TA-DA!

I don't think it worked.

No, it did not, Pointy.

Bob is more powerful than I thought.
We must try our magic on something else.

What about homework?

That is against the Magician's Code, Pointy.

Hello, Trixie! Hello, Rawrie!

We are going to make you disappear.
But do not worry, we will try our best
to bring you back.

What?

Three. Two. One.

Oh no. That teeny word makes a big mess.

It's OK, Pointy.
All magicians make mistakes, but
great magicians never give up!

SWOOSH!

We have made the wrong
thing disappear.

Yuck.

WHOOSH!

Nope.
We have disappeared
ourselves instead.

I am beginning to think magic is more difficult than we thought, Pointy.

Maybe we shouldn't do the show at all?
We might embarrass ourselves.

Do not worry, Pointy. We are
close to becoming magicians.
I can feel it.

We can do it together.

I am never embarrassed
when I am by your side.

We will go back to the drawing board.
We will use our magic skills
and our mind skills.

We will *swoosh* with confidence!

We will *whoosh* with pizzazz!

And side by side, we will make magic.

Three.

Two.

One.

TA-DA!

We have done it, Pointy!
We have learned the grandest trick!

We are ready for the
talent show tonight!

It is almost time.

Are you OK, Pointy?

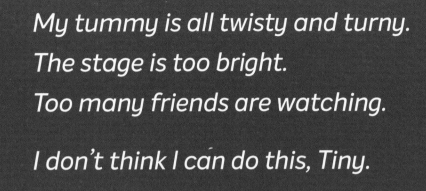

My tummy is all twisty and turny.
The stage is too bright.
Too many friends are watching.

I don't think I can do this, Tiny.

You are a great magician, Pointy. You are the
best I know! But I understand. I will try to win
this for us both.

TA-DA!!!

Sometimes the grandest ta-da is not making something disappear.

It is when someone who disappeared

bravely comes back.

Because magic is best when it is shared.

To the Amazing Jay, grateful I can make (and share) another grand "ta-da!" with you. —J. S.

To all of my teachers. —J. F.

ISBN 978-1-339-03253-5

12 11 10 9 8 7 6 5 4 3 2 1   23 24 25 26 27 28

Printed in the U.S.A.   40

This edition first printing, September 2023

Design by Jennifer Tolo Pierce
Typeset in Intelo and Brandon Printed
The illustrations in this book were rendered in pencil and colored digitally.